The Very Greedy Bee

by Steve Smallman   Illustrated by Jack Tickle

tiger tales

In a busy, buzzy beehive lived a very greedy bee.
All the other bees worked hard making honey
and cleaning the hive, but the greedy bee spent
all day gobbling pollen and guzzling nectar.

SLURP! SLURP! BURP!

The greedy bee wouldn't share his nectar with anyone.

He wouldn't even let a tired ladybug sit on his flower.

"Find your own flower!" he shouted. "This one is **MINE!**"

And when, one day, the greedy bee found a meadow full of the biggest, juiciest flowers he had ever seen, he decided not to tell **ANYONE**!

"**YUMMY**!" he buzzed. "Lots and lots of flowers and they're all for **ME**!"

The greedy bee
whizzed and bizzed from
flower to flower, slurping
and burping and growing
FATTER…

and **FATTER**…

and **FATTER** …

and **FATTER!**

At last, his tummy was full and he settled down on a big pink flower in the warm yellow sunshine and fell fast asleep.

ZZZZZZZZZZ!

When the greedy bee woke up, it was **DARK**. He tried to fly, but his tummy was so roly and poly that...

BIFF!

BANG!

THUMP!

he went down instead of up
and crashed—**BIFF! BANG!
THUMP!**—to the ground.

"**I'M SCARED**!" cried the greedy bee. "And I don't know how to get home!"

Then he saw two glowing eyes in the long grass.

"**EEK!**" he cried. "**A MONSTER** is coming to eat me!"

But it wasn't a monster. It was two friendly
fireflies, their bottoms glowing in the dark.
"What's wrong?" they asked.
"I'm too full to fly," wailed the greedy bee,
"and I can't walk home in the dark!"

"Follow us," said the fireflies, and they all
set off on the long, long journey home.

Through forests
of flowers and
squishy mud ...

over the hills and under the
stars trudged the greedy
bee. He had never walked so
far and he was very tired.

"Nearly there!"
called the fireflies.

Then they heard
the **WHOOSH** of
rushing water....

"I'm almost home!" cried the greedy
bee excitedly. "It's the stream!"
    And it was, but his hive was on the
other side of it.

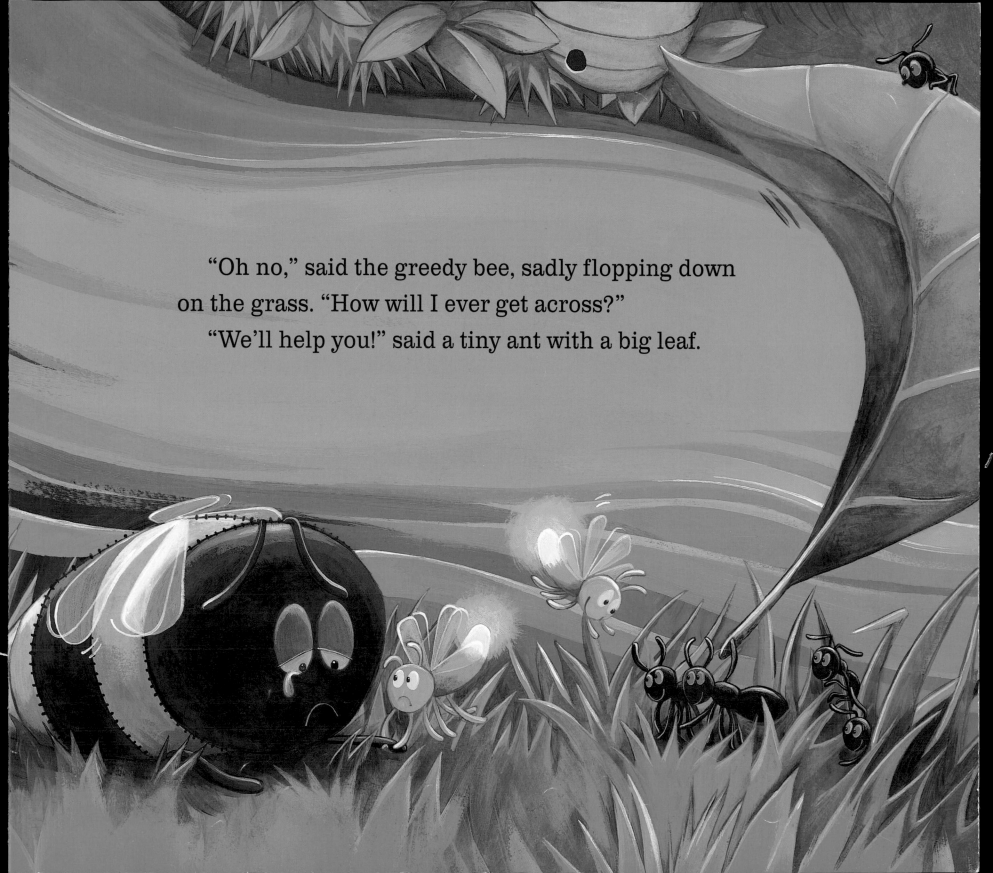

"Oh no," said the greedy bee, sadly flopping down
on the grass. "How will I ever get across?"

"We'll help you!" said a tiny ant with a big leaf.

The ant and his friends flipped
the big leaf into the water.
"Jump on!" they cried.
Helped by the fireflies, the
greedy bee and the ants made their
way splishing and splashing to the
other side of the stream.

"**HOORAY! I'M HOME!**" cheered the greedy bee.

"Where have you been?" asked the other bees.

"I **OVERSLURPED!**" said the greedy bee. "I would never have made it home if my new friends hadn't been so kind. Now I'm going to share my best honey with them. Would you like some, too?"

"Yes!" said the other bees. "Let's have a party!"

Everyone enjoyed
a midnight feast of
yummy, runny honey.
All except for one very
sleepy, very happy, but
NOT so greedy bee!